The Tough Romance

Picas Series 5

PIER GIORGIO DI CICCO

The Tough Romance

Guernica
Montreal, 1990

This is for my friends

Copyright © 1979 by Pier Giorgio Di Cicco.
Copyright © 1990 by Pier Giorgio Di Cicco
and Guernica Editions.
First published by McClelland and Stewart in 1979.
First published in this format in 1990.
All rights reserved.
Typeset by LHR.
Printed in Canada.

Antonio D'Alfonso, publisher-editor.
Guernica Editions Inc., P.O. Box 633, Station N.D.G.,
Montreal (Quebec), Canada H4A 3R1

The Editor would like to thank
Lynn Stewart and Julia Gualtieri
for their suggestions.

Legal Deposit – 2nd Quarter
Bibliothèque nationale du Québec
and National Library of Canada.

Canadian Cataloguing in Publication Data
Di Cicco, Pier Giorgio, 1949-
The tough romance
(Picas series; 5)
Poems.
Originally publ.: Toronto: McClelland & Stewart, 1979.
ISBN 0-920717-03-9
I. Title. II. Series.
PS8557.I248T68   1990   C811'.54   C88-090065-2
PR9199.3.D43T68 1990

CONTENTS

Birthday Poem for Myself, 7
Remembering Baltimore, Arezzo, 8
The Man Called Beppino, 9
Aunt Margaret, 10
Words to the Wind, 11
Summer Chances, 12
Note for a Woman at Midnight, 13
Woman, Dark Catastrophe, 14
The Head Is a Paltry Matter, 15
Growing Up in Baltimore, 16
The Elder, 17
Travelling High, 19
America, 20
After the Love, 22
The First Partita, 23
Midnight Words, 24
The Bleak Halo, 25
Maledetto, 26
Another Go, 27
The Moment I Crave From, 28
Lady, 29
Tall Stories, 30
Credo, 31
Montreal, 1953, 32
October Montreal, 33
Gioventù, 34
Returning to St. Dominic's (Toronto, 1957), 35
Willing, 36
Lying Awake, 37
Ecco, 38
The Consolation, 39
Errore, 40
Stepping Out, 41
When that Blackbird Silence, 42
Il tempo, 43
The Habit of Kicking, 44
Hard Bargains, 45
The Bird Is a Whistle, 46
The Politics of 4 AM, 47
Nostalgia, 48
Memento d'Italia, 49
Grandfather, 50
The Last Aunt, 51
Ragione, 52
Mattina, 53
Breakage, 54

The Daydream, 55
Hypothesis 2, 56
The Other Man, 57
The Ornery Tune, 58
This Is the Room, 59
String Up, 60
The Gift, 61
Sherbourne Morning, 62
Fireworks, 63
The Plaintiff in June, 64
Old Men, 65
Right Out of It, 66
Hands on the Balcony, 67
Donna italiana, 69
If I Understand Nothing, 71
Toronto-Arezzo, 72
The Men with No Chance, 74
Anniversaries, 76
Paradise, California, 77
The Dust I Have Admired, 78
The Visibility of Angels, 79
Relic, 80
The Jump on Death, 81
Aquila, 82
Canzone, 83
A Dreamer with the Usual Hands, 84
Passaggio, 85
At Home in Heaven, 86
The Unlimiting, 87
The Sundays of St. Clair, 88
Poem for My Friends and a Lady, 90
Who Will Hear of It, 91
A Straw Hat for Everything, 92
Poem from the Night Before, 93
How Happy Are the Flowers of Vermont, 94
In amicizia, 95
The Request for Air, 96
The Beaches, Lake Ontario, 97
Driving to Point Pelee, 98
Birthday Gathering, 100
Voce di luna, 101

Acknowledgements, 102

Birthday Poem for Myself

Birthday boy, your day is coming up.
There is not so much love in the whole world
as what I've saved for you.
Old pint-pot, lover of my own suit of clothes.
I am speaking from your cradle,
from the far end of your grave. And I speak
like your own mother. Be good to yourself, make sure
you've pulled your flesh up convincingly.
Make sure there's no mistake. This is the
hallowed day when you measure one morning against
another, what was and what is. Between the two
you are smoking like a mad fiend, some delinquent kid,
biding the time, half expecting the kick in the
back of the head.

Remembering Baltimore, Arezzo

The night begins slowly at first, large slow flakes
descending out of the sky's one fist.
And the bed waiting, and friends perched on
their solitudinous thrones wherever the heart
has brought them.
It seems that spring is still out of season,
the white trucks go in and out through the
darkness, the lake has the same reach night after night
a little bored with its old speech of seagulls frozen
in the dank air. There is a house not far from here, though
you would think it many miles, a house of roses, with an
old man in the front lawn, twirling his moustache,
having his last picture taken. It is my father,
before the dream blew up, of America, of uncles, older
    brothers,
of streets of gold, of Aunt Margaret and the open steel
mills kissing the harbour. It is the dream of America,
ages ago, that I run from, hiding my head in the snow,
pretending it never was, and saying yes, it should have
    started
again here, without a father's grave, with my mother
dancing lightly through the rooms of kitchen smells,
and I am nothing but a last outpost, a huge construct of
    blood
with roses that conjure houses, homes, a decent happiness.
I am not alone, I have never been alone. Ghosts are barking
in my eyes, their soft tears washing us down to
Baltimore, out the Chesapeake, round the Atlantic, round
    the world,
back where we started from, a small town in the
shade of cypress, with nowhere to go but be still again.
It is a way of saying twenty-five years
and some German bombs have made for roses in a backyard
    that
we cry over, like some film which is too maudlin to pity
and yet is the best we have to feel human about.

The Man Called Beppino

When a man loses his barbershop during the war
as well as an only son, and his wife and
daughter sing the blues of starvation, the man

believes in the great white hope, now the red white
and blue. The man ventures overseas, and lands finally
in Baltimore, Maryland, USA – destined to be the
finest barber at eastpoint shopping plaza.

That man works for nothing, because his English is
less than fine; the customers like him,
and the man is easily duped, he believes in the
honest dollar, and is offered peanuts in return.

This while the general manager runs to Las Vegas
to take porno pictures of himself between
tall whores.

The man who lost his barbershop during the war
loves great white roses at the back of a house beside
a highway. The roses dream with him,
of being understood in clear English, or of a large
Italian sun, or of walking forever on a
Sunday afternoon.

Never mind the new son, the family. It is this man, whose
hospital cheques are being spent in Las Vegas,
it is this man whose hair will shine like
olive leaves at noon; it is this man who will sit
on his front lawn, after the fifth hemorrhage, having
his last picture taken,
because he drank too much.
It is this man who will sit under his mimosa
by the highway, fifty pounds underweight, with no
hospital, and look

there are great white roses in his eyes.

Aunt Margaret

Aunt Margaret was a fat old girl
and her sons grew straight and tall and left her
in an oval world, an armchair in a house,
in a thing called planet, and her husband cursing
to an awkward grave.
But not before my misery; I see her face, that first
day off the train, taking my family home, keeping an eye
peeled to measure me against her various sons.
Knocking against the anger of twelve-year-old bones, the
grass so high I had to dream of heaven, or oceans,
to keep from taking my wrists out on myself;
I've run amuck, called growing up and running from
relations known as hell.
But still she's there.
There was a marshy patch behind her house. When Sundays
brought the family to her rooms, I'd hunt the
puddled grass for frogs and drown them in a jar, fling them
    at
walls, singe ants with glasses. Inside the house
I drowned the goldfish, choked the parakeets, and made
a paraphernalia of hell the size of those too big to kill.

Goodbye, Aunt Margaret.
I leave your frogs alone.
Your armchair sags. The pies still fill the kitchen.
Old Felix creaks his neck in metal collars.
Your sons will hardly see you. The world is growing thin,
and you grow fatter for that meat-eating world
beneath, where you can reach no one and the grass
keeps growing.

Words to the Wind

The wind rifles itself up
under the cold stars;
it fills the pockets of trees,
announces itself at my arm; I have nothing to
explain to it, a man just comes this far
under the footsteps of heaven.
I explain love, I explain death, I explain
the blood charging to my hand. No use.

It wants to see how I am doing; by entering my head,
by thinning out the bones on darkest nights.
It wants to seek me out, growing
from the eyeholes like twin flowers, to enter my
mouth and snake back out, like the words I could never say.

It wants that much.
I am waiting. And what I explain
is for the one behind me, old shyness, old friend,
boy that I was. I want you to understand what keeps
your shadow growing.

Summer Chances

Bloor Street. Mile on mile of flesh flaked off
from houses, the shops turning their tongues
in on themselves.
   A little later we find a man, trying
to sell us on a flat; he is old, and his bad English
stumbles over the tax problem. We find the trees
full of seedlings, buckets of them, they shake loose
and fall at our ears.

Why do I love you? Is it the same old heart
sitting back, waiting for a world to begin?
I am awake, as if for the first time, at five o'clock,
walking with you on Bloor Street,
the sun dying off, casting a cloud behind your head
 of hair.
The building waits, the one we call a home.
Another morning will come,
and the supper too.
But now we are walking on Bloor Street at five o'clock
in the evening. The world falls flat on its face, and we are
picking up the heaven from it.

Note for a Woman at Midnight

How shall I name these things?
Namely you. No words saved.
Shall I name you the dark you sleep in,
the star hanging over your head?
Shall I name you the walk at seven,
the touch, your silver touch on the door?

Shall I name you the love of one man
for his happiness? his refusal of a grave
to entertain the light once more caught like
a wing in your hair? I shall name you by
none of these things,

but by the anger in me, the irrefutable gist
of falling flat, right up against my life,
while you watch out for the footsteps
that would lead me further from it.

Woman, Dark Catastrophe

Woman, dark catastrophe of
my life, despoiler of the body's need,
window of bones, flesh strung together
like an afterthought, I am amazed at your
sleep, the dark riddled together to make
a thimble for your touch.

And you awake, small ghost of these nether rooms,
long sigh of these four walls, shoes ready to fit,
the dress, the air taking hold of the body's shape.

   Flame with long hair.
Imperishable one, this dull boy is all that will
become of you, his heart swelling with the words amassed
from thousands of small talks, his one tongue ribboning
the swallows of the morning.

The Head Is a Paltry Matter

The head is a paltry matter; feed it crumbs, it goes
on singing just the same.
Much too much is made of it; it goggles over a bit of
fresh wind, is perfectly astonished at the touch of love,
doesn't know what to make of itself but crosses, bearing
its own dull weight along paths it imagines have to do
with the heart.
No more of it. I'm giving it nothing to feed on.
Old lump, let it do its crossword of a grave.
You and I have better things to do, namely wrapping arms
around each other, while it hangs around, poor sot,
childlike, finding out just what it is
that lovers do, the dark between them like a clock
and their lips set to ignite one future after another.

Growing Up in Baltimore

When I think Baltimore, its grey arms
round the Chesapeake, its few crabs smouldering
in the deep. I think sadness. I think the dull glint
of steel mills in the night which is the way
Baltimore smiles. When I think of Baltimore
I think dull uncles and snarky aunts, and of the
Zellers, progenitors of my least favourite
relatives.
I think of people who do not want all their lives
to be away from Baltimore. Who have hardly heard of
 Canada.
I think long tenements, where children play at
the granite stoops. I think of hospitals
that scarcely contain their blacks, their whites,
their immigrants. I think Agnew and Joe Giordano
who ate up all my father's hospital funds in
Las Vegas. I think of a dull white house beside a highway,
a cemetery just beyond that, of a dusty mimosa in the
front yard, and my father under it.
I think Baltimore weeps for no one. It did not
love the Zellers. They didn't mind. It didn't
love my father who could never put his finger on
the ache. It didn't love me, the old bitch.
I followed her down railway tracks, behind hospitals, by
steel mills, looking for her jewelled eye, and saw nothing
but the glint of steel mills her one
charm glistening in the bay like a
mad heart, and a boy of twelve trying to
end this poem on a decent note,
with the old hag, twisting his fingers over
his face to make him look like death, with
one eye in the cradle.

The Elder

Uncle Mike, fond of the bottle,
for fifty years a recluse with a still,

charmed out of hiding for no reason.
It was his way.
    In America, he lounges on
his brother's porch.
   He is being good for two months.
when the family returns from the
supermarket one day, he will be splashing
in the basement with wine.

*

He speaks little, sleeps with his pants on
stays under the catalpa leaves in the back lot

does not dress for visitors, but stoops in the
orchard behind the driveway, in the old fedora
the sagging britches

pruning stones from the lettuce patch.
Digs slowly with the beer locked up.

Michael stares at the sun at noon
waits for the house to empty

for his binge, soils the rugs of his sister-in-law
is found belly up to the sun and happy.

*

Ah Michael. It is 1962. They will smash the still
you hide in the back lot.

In lawn chairs old biddies hear that you never
change your underwear.

Old man of the hills, they will send you back
to the old country, back to your one acre
under the vines

where, with gentle death,
tall nephews never scold you in English.

Travelling High

This is the real day; tulips mouthing the white
clouds; grass royally lined on the oak steps of an
old verandah; the walk at five or seven, the friend, the
warm coffee, the lake whispering to itself under the
dark cuffs of the city.

Heaven in an overthrow, coming in from Kingston, swung
round from New York state, down the flat line from
Baltimore nodding the Susquehanna into my dream;

old cities, crowns topped on my childhood, a woman or two,
a thousand loves. And I have never seen New Orleans no;

a touch of Florence; I dream about a cloud the size
of Tuscany, where crucifixes in the shape of fathers,
grandfathers, mortared steps, the bombs whistling
in at five or seven; there is that dream; and the

azaleas sweet on the balcony, a low wind rousing them;

and a lump of throat here, eyes washed over a city,
balconied over the hands of the lake.
I see the eyes staring back; the city keeping tab on me, and
    me
its own pulse. I have begun to see through myself this
April day, the sun has filled my pockets

and I have followed my footsteps
into the hammock of another ghost.

America

The Tropic of Capricorn someone had
left on the seat beside me, somewhere between
Utica and Albany;

Miller going on about twats
about the pasting of billboards.

In and out of bus stops, nausea in my head,
the toilet smelling at the back;
the bus jolting on freeways; nightlights
rained on the window

the night I honeymooned with America. She took
me around like a sweetheart showing off her home town.
We came upon places where Miller had had her
before me. We stepped off at depots and she was friendly
with old drunks, with sailors.

When we passed apple trees gathering frost
her eyes softened; she seemed almost childlike.
And later, tall mills, saddening her landscape, the way
a woman thinks of years with a man she couldn't love.

When we passed train yards, she reminisced about
Miller in New York, nights they made love by the roar
of trains, sparks flying at the folds of her summer dress.

The night I saw her for the first time, I saw she
was a good whore – nothing to fall in love with –
fond of the young boys who'd grown by her; tall sons
of a sort who'd go on to elegize her, claim their
corruption by her, though

no man goes on to respectable wives
after her. She was nothing to sing about, the night
she lifted her dress for me.
But quietly all over the world

her men return to their first nights with her.

Quietly, like small boys stealing apples under
furious stars,
they remember with affection

the tough romance their hands build nothing without.

After the Love

These ways do not amuse.
Nothing said, or too little.
The frozen heart, or the heart shocked
by its own silence. The walk at five or
seven is what we need, the rekindling, the
desire to stand up tall and kiss heaven
with half-parted lips, to lie down
in clean bedsheets and forget the dark coins
of the eyes. These ways do not amuse.

What amuses is the brain, the dumb beggar
with the eyes of a madman and the hands of
an angel, starting in for us and
backtracking, afraid of that hallowed
pit we have made of ourselves, that altar
and grave, where we part, and meet,
that place of every morning where we say love
and mean it, our hands shaking at the urge
to feel. The brain amuses,

what is left is parcelled off like fear,
so much drudgery, the now and again of having
grasped and missed the thing we'd kill for.

The First Partita

Damp night, breaking right through the bones.
The lights dazed off the shore.
The nighthawk hasn't entered yet.
The rooftops are filling up with the breath
of leaves.

This is a song for you, deep in your sleep,
oh lovely woman (how's that for crooning?)
it is a song that you will stay as you are,
wrapped up in the folly of our life, your flowers
mooning their odour at midnight.
There has to be a hope in hell for this thimble
our thing, what we've got left to hold on to, this
motley landscape of who it is we've been. A hope in hell
that we are the prize of each other's arms.
There is no song beyond these four walls, the breath
escaping, your eyes resting themselves in a thousand
cubic feet of darkness, the heart falling mile after
mile on a hot night, trying to recapture itself,
trying to make something up to itself.

Woman, there is a fistful of
rhetoric in my skull, see what you can do with it.
Lay it open for me in the morning, let those soft
sparrows of light collect around the three of us, the skull
and you and me.

I am saying, stay put. There is nothing to run from
and nowhere to go. Let us stay where we are, let us
amaze this rough six feet of air,
let us work out the blood to let it sound
like love.

Midnight Words

I have a love the size of Los Angeles,
the size of Los Angeles. I say it in the leaves.
I say it there and under the northern-most rock;
it is your love, woman, wrapped up in twenty feet of room;
purveyor of the body's need,
brown eyes, are you listening?
I have a love the size of Los Angeles, it is
going nowhere. I say it here, and now,
I am walking towards you, this dark night.
I bend over to kiss you. All the lights of
a thousand cities swim over our heads. A halo.
We touch, we ignite. Three years to build this cathedral,
the air. If one of us walks out, it will be with a head
full of tears.
So that I sing:
I have a love the size of Los Angeles,
brown eyes, amaze me, stay just as you are.

The Bleak Halo

The ridiculous, the want made powerful.
The need gone ga-ga. The heart flying for itself
and catching nothing.

I went away for awhile and found nothing kept still
for me to love it. So under a lamppost I saw the stars
freewheeling over my head and falling down in packages,
Xmas's without the need to tell it.

What is the size of a heart, that it is given away so quickly?
Is it the claws at the cradle, is it a man nose up to
his own shadow, is it a man with nowhere to rest his
fingers but in the folds of his brain?

What is it the lamppost says at three o'clock in the morning?
It says, you are a man come so far to try his guts on
the shape of earth, with no art to mould a god for himself;

so he stands poised, son of man, under the tender stars
    announcing
blood, the requiem of generations, in a new country, the
first place he always finds for himself, and he knows
the language will trick his mouth into saying he loves
when he doesn't mean it. What he wants is to testify
that he is strung to one star out of ten, that he goes
nowhere without dragging the whole high heaven with him.

Maledetto

How happy we are being here, the lights dance
familiarly on the lake. The balcony has its
hands full of wind –
    except that I am growing wooden;
this is because the days are blue, or wallpaper-
yellow. You did not notice that, you are too
busy eating the curtains, the light you read by,
a visit by a relative, yes well my arms
    are splintering under the soft rose of the flesh.
When I speak roses in fact emerge, roses we take
shelter in, small puffballs we climb into like
treehouses.
    This is cosy, and we have read somewhere that
this is happiness, except for my wooden legs
as if the air we breathed, the blue the violet air
were changing me.
    A long trip perhaps, or a soup, with uncles
and aunts in it.
    How do you feel about plunging long teeth into
each other to see what we are made of at this late date?
A cake, perhaps we taste of salami,
perhaps we will taste just blue just violet day, perhaps
we are two easter eggs and damned.

Another Go

High lady, moon-walker,
latecomer, runaway heart, runaway into
the hard month of October: I plead for us,
I plead that we may come out right, destroying each
other in a handhold, a star exploding between two
palms. Dark lady, I dedicate an autumn leaf, I dedicate
some footsteps. I dedicate whatever's left.
High lady, walk to me, do not sing.
Let's work this out like two madcap humans
arranging their bones beautifully. The patience,
the forgetting, the love of two shadows remembering
the noon.
When we kiss, the world whispers something about
having gone wrong, and trying to make up for us,
poor excuses for all the love in the world.
Two slapdash philosophers with the stars all over them,
making a last dash for what they thought was the sky.

The Moment I Crave From

These are the arms that can do nothing,
the irretrievable hosts,
the sticks of passion tied to the dynamite brain,
the arms that go around you, keeping you like
a last resort, while all else fails.

These are the arms that crucify me to the
shadow that I was, that walk me when the legs go lame,
that hold cups of water, that can steer the lovely sun
with a pleading look in my face.

These arms are holding you. They have come a long way
to learn to grapple a bit of air, to wrestle down
something in the shape of a heart.
These arms are all I can pray to. They are their own
conquest. When all is said and done, they will be waiting for
me, strong ropes, latched to a dump of earth.

Lady

These are the words that fail, the words clambering
up to make a synonym for you. Dove, woman,
hijacker of a dream, you.
I am done with making prayers asking that you stay
put. I want to stand stock still, see how far
you can get before the call back, the inescapable
flight of the heart going from one hand to the other.

Tall Stories

My one friend fell on his head from a fourth-floor
balcony, drunk, just in from out of town, tried to
get into his own flat by coming down the railing.

I fell on my head, he says; I look for the red bruise on
his head; he swivels in the chair, he groans, but he
always talks in groans. Here is an anecdote, he might have
said, nothing more came of it. His wife left him, either
before or after that.

There is no form to some madness. And it is not surreal.
Just the vague emptiness of people making use
of people, their lives a clanking sound of instruments
made to lever the apocryphal misfortune.

We say it at a party. He falls through the floor, we
will not be surprised, but laugh our heads off in disgust
at so much providence.

I am dying. Sure as I am sitting here, no bruises, the
great belly-laugh, god, is whispering in your ear, he tried
to make it to a cradle but got choked up on air
and walked in the grave of his footsteps. Hear it?

The dull drone of some humour, snatching the punch-line

out of your mouth and reeling you in all the while.
This is no joke.

I am alone with you; wedged between us is a slab
of hate.

Credo

The wind sharpens its teeth over the lake,
the noggin-heads, amigos wrapped in sheets, one or two
Ophelias hung by their lower lip, and the landscape oh
god the landscape I loved most spread out, over a hundred
cities, past I call it, past I died in,
I the miserable one, stuck with a flower in my mouth,
announcing the dust that is in me.

I do not believe for a minute the capacity of air for
rainbows, I do not believe that books walk in their sleep;
spring in the branches, that, for real
and the decidedly bitchy movements of thought to create
roses.

Here now, enter, coffee for you, tea, a thousand
azaleas we talk in, mash in, devour. Day outside
like any other, walk into it, into the open grave
of the air.

But I do believe in the power of bones that do not burn,
the anger of a man to stay put on the earth.
The oceans running right up to him, spewing metaphor
in pacific cups, and him turning it down believing
in footsteps that are all the metaphor of getting to a
late cradle, with a mother watching over him, with

the eyes of god and the hands of a blind man, blessing him
fiercely and cupping her tits at the stars.

Montreal, 1953

I had a dream but it's not worth the telling,
of mother's aprons sailing the clear blue air,
of the Monday wash hung out to dry, with those
white ruffians the stars filling the coal-black night.

And the dream was of a verandah, six miles above
the earth, of a white cat in the barnyard of my fun,
a fat man with the smile of Jesus selling me hope
to ply my way through this witless world, and me with not
sense enough to close my eyes and cry for the boy I was.

October Montreal

Se fa dopo le persone dotte.
(The learnéd ones will come later.)

Montreal is damp and blue this month.
Artie Gold walks the streets, out of love with his lungs.
The wind is from the oak trees of Mount Royal.
The cross bows towards the river, and the buildings, they
will live forever.

I walk to the childhood at St. Zotique.
On Dante Street is the bust of Dante, stern in the sun,
on a little square. A woman and a child play in the October
leaves. The world is evacuated.

Under the church de la Défense the wind turns on itself.
In 1921, the bust went up; *Se fa dopo le persone dotte,* the
inscription reads.

My father, impressed by nothing but a touch of home
saw Dante Street, perhaps that sign that reads "Toscana
   Furniture,"
heard a familiar sound, and called the rest of us to join him.

Twenty-five years later, I leave him under lilacs near New
   York.

The St. Lawrence still flexes its fingers towards the ice floes.

The wind flaps at my trousers. October Montreal is damp
and blue. Leaves are falling on the woman and child. She is
   on
hands and knees, in black and wears a scarf. She is
   whispering
in his ear the handhold of all those who are lost in their own
language; he hears the wind.

I hear *se fa dopo le persone dotte.* I walk towards the town,
the sky on three sides of my brain, in between I am learning
   a new
language, always a new language. Like Artie, I am sick of
my lungs.

Gioventù

That was the real hosannah
in the playground at noon,
the baseball bat levelled at a cloud
the sun thick in the hands;
a few blades of grass blowing into a patch of blue.

And me with not horse-sense enough to run
out of the day, nor sense enough to freeze,
to stay put, to become the charm of the
age –

a boy, kept still by his own devising
and outright fright at the years creasing his hands,
and the blue crammed in at his mouth like so much
   dynamite
set to explode at the sound of a kiss.

Returning to St. Dominic's (Toronto, 1957)

The playground in the dead of night; old buildings cleared
away; I assume the black-top is the same on which I bled
the first kick by an upstart boy;
the old nun, the one who'd throw me out, stands
on the gateway steps, chiding my mother, whose bad
Englishes make mincemeat of my will to live.

Angela, Maria, Vincenzo, romances, all my
loves and hates; you've gone to hell, I know it
for giving a rough time to an angel.

Talons at my heels, let's say; but that prime time
was flawless except for you.
I alone exist, small ghost on a black-top, rehearsing blood
flows, embarrassments, the dark sky growing darker
in my chest. On the corner of this street and that

the sadness begins. Remembering the bony toil of seven
    years
of childhood, a grown man stands here. Having made
his leap away from Christ, the fool, he chokes those
culprits of a tender age.

The playground echoes with the jeers and holler.
These should be blood stains and the signs of
dreaming gone berserk, instead of footsteps

leading me to a safe bequest, another month, another
home, with all the years like burrs stuck in my side.

Willing

That black apple the sun is dead,
mouthfuls of it taken, by poets,
lovers, the inebria of scuttlefish,
joe blow; all lamenting the sun, all a praise of
the sperm-god sun; all a wishful May-dance
around that rooter of lilies, the sun; oh world

plum of an afternoon, unhinge from it, sail yourself
through dark; open the way you do in my head, say
at 3 AM; you do not need a sun; you need
the cartilage of my need to make you hang well.
Where would you be without me? I have done with praising
the exterior villains of a rutabaga world; that sharp fist
your heart is hung right through to a dream I had
of children, their moth eyes filling the gardens with
delight, the warheads emptied from their hands.
It is the same dream I propose to you: love this boy,
blue-eyed and fair, do homage to his excellent exercise
of keeping you fit for a lifetime.

Lying Awake

Disease. Disease called brain is sitting on the
left side of the skull.
The song is a nutshell. I tire of making it hold.
The lake. The lake takes you easy, it is a repetition of last
year's sob-meat. Old men go crying in the streets. It is the
rehearsal of one foot in front of the other.
Bravo. The old dance step, I have learned it backwards.
So much of me has learned to be without the other half.
Now that the woman leaves me, in the body that breathes
　caves where
once sparrows tongued the light out of me,
it is that plain; it is that simple. The bat, the head, hovers
　above
my sleep – the old grail without the blessing. The love of one
year out of a hundred like a sword, cold against my
　numbest side.

Ecco

Love breaks where no light shines,
this is the dark heaven;
the real thumbnail;
the rain of sadness,

the heart strung up to that hammock, the grave.
The sadness of one man, arranging footsteps
backwards into his life, picking up dead things,
annoying himself with the splendour of unreal things;
and the man cries, too
he cries to fill the rooms. The absence of good,
the healthy rebuttal of one thought against another.

The man forgets things, like hands at the touch
of a rose, a wide leaf in the eyes of sunlight;
if he leaves, no one will hear him;
pathos has no use for itself;

this song is made up of three terrors;
one is the terror of self;
one is the terror of others,
one is the terror of having loved and missed it;

the last one is like thorns in his head;
the rose without the petals to deflower,
he walks, buffoon, charming existence out of
the simplest loss.

The Consolation

This is the consolation of writing verse.
The academic thimble. Drink up.
But I am alone in the dark. The sign says, nothing like
what it was; this is the new shit-hole, the walls that
must be made into gold. You will recognize nothing.
There are new names the size of footsteps, graves you
must scour to step into at once, the little manger
where the world seems right, where the lid closes, all
    depending
on the grace you make of yourself.

Errore

We talk of old men who have forgotten their
thoughts, of old women with cancer like
sponges at the face. We say how medicine
doesn't know anything, how we can croak
because the mystery in us
gets teeth. Fear opens its little satchel,
a small bat flies off into the head.

       I want to live for many years like a stone.
I want to announce the end of the body's partnership.
I want to enter a small tunnel not big enough
for my flesh,
       I want to arrange a song and dance for me
and death, laughing it up as the bones cart
their old clothes out the door.
       I want to live forever in the eye of a needle.
I have no footprints, I lied about them.
My mother is not getting old. It is a bad joke,
one day she will walk out of the machine of
sinew and heart and say – it is all right, you can come
out now, god is sorry for the wrong wrapper.

Stepping Out

I walk into the Sunday rain,
your emptiness follows, all you've taken away
clods behind me, the dead luggage of a hundred years
of kissing right, of a tender moon, all wizened for
a bit of heartbreak.

The leaves are getting heavier with the late fingers
of autumn. The sky grows thinner. I have imagined
all sorts of fools this month. I have a patience for
them all. I grow tidy with my own uselessness.

My feet walk me to this plot of grass, now that.
I am elated by the simple fashion of making it home.
There is so much rain, the avocado has lost its leaves.
The wall grows whiter, there is a wall that grows
whiter. Everything can be made out to be a little hell,
a paraphernalia of putting things wrong in an okay world.

I am hanging by my own limbs. Choking on the fresh air
of having grown right, by coming down hard on
what I can't believe in – one arm around the
marker of hope, and the other arm waving for dear life,
on a usual day, making a run for it,
in the distance that was ours once only.

When that Blackbird Silence

Certain parts of the body are falling off.
The weather cannot touch me.
My hands drop off at the touch of flesh,
my head drops off on the pillow,
my legs will not stand me up,
but the heart has learned to fly.
It is a little marvellous and stupid watching
its acrobatics, from a distance deep as a grave.

It is a little wishful thinking. I call it that.
When my legs fall back together, my arms
rejoicing at the knot of bone, my footsteps learning
one another, the nest made ready,
my heart will be tired out.

It has followed virtually every move you have made,
loved one; I am carrying this crutch, the body, around,
I will have to make up names to persuade it all is well.

I have to get the timing right.
A shadow is a long thing to lie down in.
It is a long time between one day and another.
I have to keep the bones together, this once,
I have to make up wings, I have to persuade myself
one sky is as good as another. I have to talk to
myself, to call back what I have let escape –
another hope, its mouth crammed with sprigs.

Il tempo

We are reduced to thinking of time, and its slow
    machinations,
its front teeth, back teeth, backed up to a baby's smile,
up to love's door, up to the divan, look! Now it is serving
coffee, now it is putting you to bed; time eats
the simplest things, the ties, the books and gets around
to your skin, and sits in the left hand of your brain

and says, spit out the love you knew awhile ago. Time comes
in carrying bandages; here's for your eyes; time tells you
anything to keep you. Losing time,

like in this poem, we see our hairs stand up on end, in
an impossible thunder. Losing time, we forget nothing;

everything is as it should be remembered. The beautiful
    baby
it was, before the wind stole it. Time enters with the end of

this poem, and looks ridiculous.

The Habit of Kicking

You step out the door and you fool me every time.
Thinking you will come back with the world right
on your shoulders, smiling continually, wishing me well,
seducing me with a last gasp of how things could be.

I am learning better. Nothing makes more sense than
the heart brought up proper
to be knocked into sense by the loss of things.

I am learning every time to lie still and let the world wash
   over.
But I get up at the last minute
and botch it by trying hard to stay viable as a living thing,
I throw my arms out and botch the morning air, announcing
a last ditch effort to love, keeping
no secret alive, I tell the world, I am making it one more
   time,

into that circle where a man laughs at himself,
for the thousandth time, while his bones lead him
on in the good humour of another year.

Hard Bargains

These are the hours that kill,
the fade-aways, the hard passions
grown pin-sized, the flaking off
of three thousand years of making
the heart grow right, for a parcel
of empty rooms, for a little wind entering
through the window,
the dead wood of desire staring you in the face.

There is only one man lonelier than me,
it is the shadow I call brother, lunatic,
winner and loser of his own suit of clothes.
Charmer of the body's need, despoiler of old
footsteps, father of my own children. He is the evil

of a man watching himself grow, locked against the
four walls of his goodness, amazed at his own reflection,
counting fingers; he is the last effort of a dream,

he is the dog I have looked for all these years.
He neither sits up nor lies down.
I have grown used to barking at my arms,
shouting myself out of another reach.

I see myself vaguely, the runaway, the beaten thing,
the tail between my legs, the fond heart with the whispers,
the old dream kept alive by killing off the new.

The Bird Is a Whistle

There is no use in thinking these things out.
The heart goes on flopping in its tiny box.
The balloon of the lungs goes on filling
with garden air.
      The head, soft contraption, is making
sentences of a woman's arm,
      and I am making dance steps
to an open field, not yet opened up with
grave-plots.

I will sit around and watch the world hatch
with its own marvel; something in me has seen
this before; the love that is good once only,
the thought that brings down its flag on a rainy
afternoon, the baby's cry that is like a string of
stars, the gibberish understood
by a maddening god.
      I will sit around and watch the leaves
do their fantasia of getting green.
I have a pact with my bones.
I tell them nothing
and they walk me to your house.
Only at night I whisper terrible reproofs,
the last anger of a man watching himself grow,
dreaming his way, like birds against
hard walls; while his heart stands still,
long dead, the beautiful cadaver the air
keeps praying to.

The Politics of 4 AM

The fly caught in the cupboard. All those
cookies hurrah, let him choke on them.
I locked him up in there, tired of chasing him.
The towel wet with falling in the kitchen sink.

There are the blue girls, spring in the branches,
Easter celebration, a plate of pasta,
and a fly caught in the cupboard.

The general too, throw him in, he is locked up
in the ribcage of sleep in white walls, old fly,
buzzer, goofball with the wings tied to his girth.

Primavera. The poems are nodding off to sleep.
A button goes off in Moscow. I clap like a gleeful
child in a cave of snow. This began a long time
ago, this dancing in the house of cards.

Now I am marching down a thin white road,
now the moon falls on my lap. A fly in a cupboard.
What is the name of the loneliest thing alive?
Amigo? Are you listening.

This grave I am singing right to the end.
Mouth it, the words come by memory. It is the song
of death, and the dancing you have just made up.

Nostalgia

The sunlight dashes in from the lake
in large armfuls, stretches itself on
the room; some clouds are putting the lid
on the western light.

It was so brief, and I am thinking still of
summer; the snow rags the streets, a little bit of
wind wraps the cold bones of the maple.

And now it is waist-high grass in
Michael's orchard, the slender cypress on the hill
beside Bruno's house, the light taking small
steps over the Tuscan hillsides, pines,
and the green lizards basking beside the
cathedral.

I am obsessed with warmth, is it not common,
even here friends are a premium; I would think
they'd run head first into the love of friends,
they suffer everything else.

The lake is warming its hands, but fails; more snowflakes
ditto in from a low cloud, the light draws itself
in on the farthest sky.

Italia, far beyond that, always, Italia
and the rooms of warmth, the landscape searing
its edges at noon.

Under a few cold lilies, my father dreams
cicadas in Vallemaio. I am sure of it.
He left me that, and a poem that is only a

dream of cicadas; the brown glove widens
on the dry December earth.
I am a little marvellous, with the sunken
heart of exiles.

Memento d'Italia

In Arezzo, at the railway station,
there is a café-restaurant that looks onto
the tracks; at mid-day the train yards simmer
like a mirage. It is a small room with white
table cloths, a palm tree in the corner
and very few come there, and do not stay long.
And this place had changed little. In Arezzo
there are few places like this. Once I saw this
I came there every day, to learn images unrazed
by German gunfire. I sat there and ventured my eyes
at random on the passers-by, pig-tailed girls lugging
a suitcase, lovers leaning together while the
trains lumbered in and fumed. And most valid, the
noon sun, searing the air, waving up from the trains.
Of this, I was most sure; and took it with me
as if to say, this is what my father saw, however
many years ago, and there must have been a time
when there was nothing more on his mind than the
air like a mirage, the passers-by, perhaps that
potted palm and the afternoon just waiting.
This I brought back with me.
An affirmation.
Much that went between this man and I is changed.

Grandfather

I heard the story once.
How the Nazis grabbed you by
the balls and scruff of the neck
and tossed you out the window
two floors. I remember wondering
if you died of shock, the pain
or the splash of bones.

You were a kind man, lazy
and unwitting. I got that much from mother.

You'd done no harm. A little hen-pecked
with a second wife who lived out her days
gloating over her old age.

I saw photographs. You were short,
moustachioed, noble with indolence.

You must have been asleep when
they caught you that morning, and killed you
for sport. I grew up seeing you killed
in your photograph suit, all tidy

and packaged for death, small, an easy
handful for two black uniforms.

Always you at the window, poised
for a swan dive

surprised in your sleepiness
the pain waking to the dumb fall.

Just two men, emptying a house
of people. The rest of the family
went through the front door
in their heads the memory of you
caving in for years.

The Last Aunt

She is eighty-five.
Here she comes onto the lawn, under full stars.
Led out by an only nephew, who comes and spreads
her bones delicately in a long chair.

A fine tired woman, her mind gone, gibbering lonely
things as she descends in his arms.

She sits with us, family and friends, as we talk politics,
weather; she will straighten her collar the
whole time, the air above her turning with elm leaves.

So often someone remembers her there,
gives her a gentle tug on the sleeve, and she smiles,
brought back from somewhere.

She is poked fun at, to keep ourselves from crying.
We are sure she remembers laughter.
If she is cold, it is because we tell her so.
If she is tired, it is because it is time to come in.

I saw her eyes by daylight, bright and lost in everything
she sees, now they are hiding in the cuffs of night.

When we turn away, her ears fill emptily with
the sound of crickets.
The wind misses her in its long hands.

Very soon someone will tell her she is gathering
apples, and she will pick the pebbles at her feet
and roll them gently, in the folds of her dress.

Ragione

One more heaven out of nothing. Practising right
to make a chance bloom from the throat.
I understand that my lungs are brushing up
to each other, to make a bit of night-music.

To make the legs walk straight, to make sense of
the cups of sun, to make the shade a little darker to rest in.

So much beauty made ready for. I lie down in a place of my own
forgivings, tagged to the tail-end of my days,

trying the door of the body's strength,
and falling under it. The panic is old-hat.
There is that newer day for which the body repeats
its favourite sayings, charming away its
old wounds. Bandaged, it walks right up to
an early sun and makes a gift of itself, hoping to trade
in something in the shape of a heart for a stay in this world.

Reprieve is such a casual thing. It comes with flowers,
it comes with trusting yourself to make the best
out of nightfall; it comes with a friend, or it comes
with making your right arm sprout music, just to fill
a room with the sound of being alive.

That much power, just for growing up, saying bye-bye
to the tall son that you were and entering your father's
clothes, the elegies flaking like thread as you
walk along.

It is the old suit you are saying goodbye to. The bony
toil of the hands strung together to make an embrace.
If you lie down now, you will have admitted nothing.
And that is the sour end of staying around,

the mean habit of breath without a need for song.

Mattina

I'm a little tired of the all-out leeching,
this good time, not meant, this eight-month explosion
called getting up in the morning to find a replacement for
my chest. I'm not the wild son-of-a-gun that made
your arms out to be wreathes, out of which happiness
    popped its ugly
head, that happiness that hit the roof, the clouds; did it hit
anything? I saw it climbing the window the other day, all

its mouths agape. It sang nothing – just mouthed, I couldn't
    make
the words out for limbs, eyes, a walk to the garden.

Now I'm sending back to your place a parcel of explosives,
I'm sending you three ghosts that gnaw at your floorboards,
that carry you off in their burning arms. I'm not sure what
    happens
after that.
But let's begin again. I'm after you as a last resort, the sure
    killing,
the reinstitution of parts. My smile, flying back to me, its
    legs mended.

This is the effort of giants,
of small furry things. This is how the world turns on itself,
painfully, gripping the dark, falling on morning
every god-forsaken time.

Breakage

This is the centre of the universe, the black hole,
the irresponsible foetus, the black tear of the head,
in my own pocket, the feet that will not go moonwards.

Oh woman, you have done this dreadful thing, the acrobatic
heart lunging at itself, and splaying itself on roses.

Your house turns to putty, your house turns to cake,
your house turns to anything, but the fire burns in me, the
   fire
to absolve my merriment, that crazy remembrance of two
lovers in the snow.

This song breaks open in three places, the last of which
is your smile, that pendulum crazy over my bed. I want
to kill you, it is that simple. But I also want to find
a replacement for that cotton-mouth, my love.

The Daydream

I want to say a few words regarding myself,
this chatterbox, this skull full of teeth,
this lie-awake wonder on pins and needles,
this disaster with eyes on fire,
this word-user that believes the world can grow on two sides
with his heart in the middle.

I believe he's left home, he left his home burning
with a cigarette. He always expected it. He's found love
to be a bit of an overnight thing. He's on the
Atlantic using his arms like oars. He's on a campaign
to pull his heart up from the ocean floor.

I don't understand why the closet door didn't say goodbye to
me when I left. There's no feeling in the simplest things.
I'm expected to believe in sidewalks. I don't believe in

anything but the storm of my hands over the Atlantic floor
scraping portraits up, that look like hearts, people, syringes.

If I come back now what will I be? Will the flesh keep still?
Will the hat fall out of my head with the dwarf under it?

Hands, why do you cry, woman, why do you come back?
I see myself over and over again, and what I behold is two
   sheaves
of wheat trying for the sun, burning with the earth inside
   them
burning, oh my love my eyes are on fire, and the Atlantic

is not big enough for a thimble.

Hypothesis 2

Wisdom is the hat of the old. Don't want it. Take the
forgiveness back, I'd rather your lips, the smile flung against
the broken moon, the bleeding. Over again, I'd have it be.
Not this place, this leaving of conclusion, the questions with
no answers, the lack of blame, the anger of no justice in
the world.
I'd rather the heart in a tea cup, spending. The true
 heroism,
the making of big fuss over nothing to keep the blood
 flowing.
          That simple.

I will forgive you nothing, to stay ready for the next time
the tap on the shoulder says, look love, one more heaven,
open your mouth and sing.

The Other Man

It was last year, this time, we met,
old caboodle of the heart's flim-flam,
lover of one suit of clothes, betrayer, dark savager
of that little cup, our love.

And what have you to show for it? Something we made
is lying face down, eating a grave.

Our footsteps together. The way the moon fell on your
    shoulder
in November.

I've left you, the incompatible doo-dah.
Another friend by the wayside, because a heart dropped
    from your hands.

Because your head fell over in the botch-up of figuring out
    the brain.
Because the leaves fall, and it has nothing to do with either
    of us.

I've left you. I stepped out of my lapels.
I signed your name on closet doors.
You took a woman from me. I found you in three thousand
cubbyholes breaking the crucifix of your arms.

There is no time for the make-up. A chest the size of Los
    Angeles
breaks over the ocean, and the word grief falls.

Why have you come so late, in the manner of lynching the
    heart?

The Ornery Tune

I will not forget your anger, your leaving,
your foot-tread, lady why do the October leaves
begin newly, they fall, into the caverns of eyes and destroy
children; destroy for example the thousand-year-old men
who loved you, sent packing.
They come back, wizened beards, asking the whys, the hows,
the new day, they are always asking after the new day.

No answer. I've got suitcases for them, packed, ready to go
to the moon, to the next block, to the next arm; they
come back, the wizened men, and they have nothing to say.
  Huge
flowers are falling from their beards. Playgrounds ring in
  their heads.

Roads are burning. They do not hear, they do not know a
  world
beyond your own. When will you give them the passports,
the go-aheads, the saying that it is all right? One love is not
a place of being still. Cut off their balls, make them jump
at the rain, make them anything but old men. They believe
  in
themselves when you aren't looking.

This Is the Room

This is the room without fail,
the place that kills, where the roses fly up against the walls.

This is where habit breaks itself, the lovely habit
the bad habit. All goes.

I am growing two hearts in this place.
One waits for spring. One is eating a song.

I stand, a little to the right, watching.
I had not made provisions for the tear falling out of my head.
I have made up some blood to make it look like blood,
to fool it into flowing.

Everything is as it should be, explicable, a little rough.
No one should walk in at this point.

No one.

String Up

String up this dead
thing, me, with the words sewn
on to his lip,
old fancy pants,
long-time wooer of all that goes sour fast,
blood-letter, and good at it,
amazing symbolist of touch,
string me up; I am good at blocking the sun,
a little shade for the tiny leaf;
some children under it,
a fast planet below that, and between all, dust
teething the footsteps of the young;
string me up, there's no time to lose;
let us use things well: I proffer myself, first progeny
of all that goes to the grave fast, poet and dream-maker,
I admit the usefulness of all those who haven't
the heart to stand and watch; no cop-out,
I want to make marvellous use of what mother gave me:
six feet of bone, at last, with that necklace the sun
trading us in for the dark.

The Gift

The world pulls down its pants
and he's at it, doing the most remarkable
things
he would not do to himself; that's what the
world is for, a way of touching
himself in places
sacrosanct, impossible
to bear.

Sherbourne Morning

I begin to understand the old men, parked on benches
smoking a bit of July, waiting for the early
bottle; the large tears of the passers-by, wrapped
in white cotton, the world bandaged at 7 AM;
        when the day goes old, they lean over
and nod into their arms, lovers, one-time carriers
of their separate hearts; their wives, their children
are glass partitions through which they see themselves
crying. Love them, or better yet, imagine a world
without a footstool for the creased and lame; imagine how
    that
sun above them spins halos for angels gone berserk.

Fireworks

The fireworks pop off
on the sleeve of the lake.
The white buildings cowering beside it;
a thousand noggin-heads asleep, this side of
New York State, and me, strung by those tremendous
ropes of air, my lungs, clapping existence out of a meaning.

There is the blue grass I imagine by
the shore, a love the size of a heart torn up
with wanting, the editorial offices burning their yellow
   flame,
the cars kissing their fenders against a whitewashed moon.

Tomorrow is a claptrap, with me, face against friends,
the long white arm performing miracles of reaching
into water and coming up with clocks. The walk
into a cave of sun where nothing sings but the body reaching
out in all directions, the notes hung up to dry in
that hooker of limbs, the air.

I want to lie down now, and become a field.
That the moon will not see me.
Let the nighthawks pass me by.
Let me imagine that I am here by my own becoming,
that I was not born a crucifix to my own plot of ground.
Let me be grass, the wind in my hair, let me arrest

the fireworks over the lake. Suppose they light upon
my own dark thoughts, let me fill the mammoth
skull of night with speech until the lilacs go charging
from the eyeholes, peering at god through his own dull gaze;

let me imagine that the earth is what I leap from,
that we are here as trees are, all leaves above the chin
and roots of dust.

The Plaintiff in June

The air darkens. It begins to rain.
Some birds keep at it in the maple tree.

Some months ago Stanley Cooperman put
a bullet through his head, rearranging the dust
that used to explode in words.

Now he is singing angels in a nether tree.
The land is a dull moan, drizzled on.
The trucks go on whizzing tying cities together
as if some stockyard meat were the essence
of seventy years of staying.

I think of you Stanley, and a cup spills from my hand,
a cup of a thousand small songs that spill and grow nothing.
I want to arrange a dawn for you tomorrow, one you
can talk to, one big enough to persuade you not
to make your body a raintrough for the stars.
I am putting enough words into that dawn, though you
can't hear it, to keep us covered forever,
like a heart that has not the courage
to go naked unless it dress in the fire
of the tongue shooting to bring down
one heaven after another.

Old Men

The old men have their glories
on cool verandahs, on rocking chairs
on britches, with the large hats.

In front of them, by the corn-stalks
the day goes by slowly, carting what
remains of young arms,
the flush of kisses.

Even now they do not see dusk
edging up to the barns from the low fields.
It scares only the children, the oldest ladies.
The old men, they will have it come and
sit with them at steps, on cool verandahs

and they will gibber a bit, as if the dark
understood, confiding an embrace or two,
a long journey, the large apples of an
uncle's orchard. Their faces in the porch
light are like the day saying
its last words between two birches.

Right Out of It

I make use of every tear-jerker, oh lady love,
fled one, skinny-minny with a heart full of silences,
remember this dull boy

the insistence of a flower on his arm,
the commendable stone's throw of a smile reaching
another. I am the four walls of my happiness

the last-ditch effort of getting up in the morning
I am not least of all the autumn leaf
trying to make its way backwards, the friend-gatherer
with a centre of hurt.

I climb up my own arms into that tender room my
brain, where I make up stories about two children
with the sun right up to their mouths, flailing
around in an April air, one heaven after another.

I'm so many words without an ending. I'm the way it came,
that barrelling of disaster, only to come out a man with an
　　extra tear in his head.

I lie down and become what I want to be. It is that easy
with the windows of love wide open, a thousand cubicles
of grief flapping their wings at another morning.

Everything is possible now. Every time you begin
there is an angel with sharp wings beating the ribs
into place. It is neither a good angel nor
a bad angel, it cups my bones like a shadow.

It's already twelve miles up, and I'm shouting it down
like a runaway dream I want to catch up to.

This time I'm going to skip twice before falling.

Hands on the Balcony

We will remember this;
the blue moon in the right hand, the stars dimpling
out of the west heaven, the love parked not two doors
away, the remembrance of what it was to grow right,

to have become mamma's boy, to destroy the world in a
  handhold.
There was never a man we could have grown into.
We came this far out of a simple prayer, the closet of terrors
we grew hair to get out of, the cities lapped by our shining
sides. The nightmare of darkness we ran from; remember it,

it's still the only way to clear nightfall.

Now I am standing here with my right lung perched to an
  autumn
air. I am remembering how love defeats itself to grow
  mouths.
I have to talk this out. I have to discuss with myself how I've
come this far to have lost everything.
How could I run so fast?

There are lakes and oceans, sons and daughters we have
  never
dreamt of, a thousand fields we could lie in. There's the trust
of your own feet stalking themselves. There's mother's
  portrait

tacked to the far wall. There's father's moustache nodding,
  a little
flower hung from a star. There's that first lap,
there's the raking arms of children knocking the sense out
  of you,
there's the lover you gave the box of your heart to.

There's the city. You wanted it. You took it by storm.
Now you start again, all ten fingers flinching. It is autumn.
But it could be summer as well. This is the third time you
  have

begun. Dust your arms off, and say love again, this time stretch the
lips out, take in the whole heaven, and spout out the heartless stars.

Donna italiana

Lady, I cannot help myself in you. There is the
song of three thousand years, of little old men with the
eyes of saints, they walk on the hillsides in the mid-day
  heat,
ghosts, wishing me well. They are my grandfathers, and my
  great-grandfathers,

and the ancient men that kept my ribs burning at Monte
  Cassino, in the
air above my brother's corpse, in the shelled house in
  Arezzo, in

Rimini, where I sat spread-eagled on the sand; they kept
  the ribs
burning through the cold Montreal nights, and in
  Baltimore, behind the
cold hospital where my father died. The ribs burned all the
  nights of my

life, my gentle men, my grandfathers, ghosts in the hills
  behind
Arezzo, burning their gentle eyes at night. Woman, I touch
  you

and remember everything, you open your mouth and laugh
  and I hear the
wind in trees beside the cathedral, the wind that weeps at
  nothing,

running through my shirt, past the skin I have devised for
  myself,
to the ribs, and the ribs sing, cooling. You are that much

gentleness. Yours is the only laughter that can persuade me.

It was that day upon the hilltop, I looked down over the
  parapets
of my town, into the hand of noon; hives of sun over the
  rivers,

pathways I imagined over distant slopes, farmyards
    kneeling over the fields
of grass, behind me the scent of pine from the public
    gardens; at that

precise hour, I heard you, I felt you toss your head back,
    and your laugh
persuaded me. Like the country of my youth. I cannot help
    myself

in you. Only you persuade me that the hills were white.
    Only you
persuade me that the ribs burn less and only when a
    woman is

the country that I love.

If I Understand Nothing

I feel the need for you come over me, in a matter of short
    days,
you are there as you always were. There is the vast
    suspicion,

you are the country of my birth and all the swallows of the
    town
where I was born, and all the dawns I saw from the
    campanile even

when I was three thousand miles away. My Roman beauty,
    you bring to me
all my childhood songs with the colour of dark hair. For you
    are the poems

I always wrote, for you, the makeshift monuments made for
    other women.
These are the notable tears that were to set me sailing to
    the land

of giants, where I slew everything for the price of nothing.
I come back through the door behind me, and find new
    furniture,
new places for the cost of love, I build a house of breath, and

return in it. This is the place in the world that pays homage,
donna, I subscribe to your eyes, for now and always. As you
    were

always here, I return you to myself.

Toronto-Arezzo

I miss you not at all, woman, misery-maker, despoiler
of three years of happiness. The snow falls tonight, and it is

the end of nothing. It is two years almost since you clubbed our
apartment to death with a little finger. It is two years almost that

my heart has grown double the size of this city.

*

In one continent they believe that if you are not happy once,
you amend the circumstances by leaping. They believe in fairy tales
(I have heard this all the way from California) that people are

mourning over the death of good times, by going it alone.

In one continent if two people are not happy over the course of
two weeks, they begin to gnaw at each other from the insides,
until they fall apart like pieces of wood. These are the great

romantics that see heaven in a walnut.

*

There is a town so many miles away. Where people stick to the earth
like trees and are not amazed if they

should flower twice in one season. This will sound romantic.
In one continent they would laugh at this, yet toss in their
sleep. There is a town so far away, that laughs at itself

for saying so, and moves on.

*

Woman, I have lost so little sleep this week, that I wake up
in my home town, having lost nothing. If you should be sorry

at any point, it is the story of two continents, one too far
   from
the other. The flowers are drifting shoreward to your feet. I
   have
gone. The campanile from my home town rings. I have gone

home, where I dreamt one night of an English city and an
   English love.

The Men with No Chance

These are the men with no chance. The dreamers
with one arm open, with the guitar and the brandy and the
thousand and one songs for every occasion. The snow keeps

falling; it is the Christmas of their lives. There are no
 packages for
them. They have opened themselves again and again,
 having
found love, deep as a mile, having spent their arteries

on the kiss, having gone out, having delivered the world
to themselves. They have been visiting forever.

Tonight is only another night such as they have always
 loved.
If they go to midnight mass it will be to recapture animals

as only children can. These are the men of grief and all
loveliness such as they dream of on the Grecian islands,
 such
as the islands they dream of in the dark hair of a woman;

these men have had children, that live now in the most
 incredible
homes. These men will burn their house down out of ritual
 one
morning, with not one loss more. They will dedicate this one

to you, should you walk in the door. Your Christmas to
 them is the
specialness of your youth, which they will wear like an

amulet, they have so much to ward off. The men with no
 chance have
the largest eyes in the world, and their eyelashes are
 sometimes
long, their reach is something that never ends, their grasp

is less than likely; when they embrace, bombs go off in the
chest, something like flowers falling on the kitchen table.

There is nothing too specific or dramatic about it. They remember
autumn because it meant the spring. They remember you like the last

chance before they could have lost it. They have nothing to do with
your beginning. They want you as if clouds had gone between

two hills, without touching the flowers. The shadow and the
raindrop is all you will remember when you have forgiven them.

Anniversaries

For the thousandth time, you walk back in.
Neither of us is fooling the other. We love, unequivocally,
every part of each other. I will love you until the end of time
and it will kill us. We will find ourselves in a grave, hands
tied to each other, the lilacs of our own mouths de-petalling
the word love as we have for years. Nothing can make us go
away. We have done so, come back, and found our eyes like
  poles
in a winter snow lighting up nothing but the heart again.

This can never be reduced. We loved too well just once, may
  never live
it down, we will go on mistaking the sun for each other's
  names,
on the tip of the tongue always that one that taught one
  love.

Even the words come back to me now, the namesake of
  what they
were meant to be, not who they were meant for.
Less than perfect, too perfect, we are the unhappy. We will
  never live
together again, and always be homeless for each other. The
  lump
in the throat laughs at itself. Whatever love could manage it
  couldn't
manage itself, to tie its shoes and say good morning.

So we go on meeting in cafés like this, one hand in the other.
The world revolves, and we can never get on. Tonight I will
  sing
to you in the darkness. You are the only person to
  understand this,
there is always a new kind of loneliness, for every new kind
  of innocence.

Paradise, California

My little California girl, you write back,
madness, saving itself from a paper bag, you write
the blue sorrows on your lover's brow, you write me

the responsibility of a human being for another, and you
tax a simple decency. I have always begun in myself,
ending up in other people's hands;

the blue moon came down from the sky for breakfast
one day; I don't remember if it was Alabama
or Saskatchewan; my fingers wrapped themselves around

that mouldy moon like the song of a man, like the sticks
of a cradle. Tires fall forwards from cars, loiter
at my feet, and expect that I will turn them into
sparkles.

The only way the bandage of the body wraps itself
is with a strong thumb on the heart. There are no
sidestreets to hide in, my twenty-year-old wonder. The

bed is twice as long every night. Hope to grow into it,
there are no handouts. Love can't cherish what it can't relax
   for.

I am on stilts, five thousand feet in the air; if I
look down, I see your hair, so soft, I want to

touch it. That much care is higher than clouds,
further off than hope.

The grass grazes in itself. It is time you flew.

The Dust I Have Admired

How many restaurants. I am tired of all the
restaurants, and the discussion of women gone berserk,
and the delicate wine, and the ride home, or the stop-off
at the bistro, the espresso, the French women mooning
their eyes over candles.
Death sings itself in me, death and the fact that two
people can destroy their love
over nothing but time, they can make mincemeat of a smile,
they can do this and live on like blackbirds.

Two legs, two arms, two hands, let's have the roster,
let's call up all the parts. How they sleep together
at night. Let's note the throw-aways, the beginning and the
end, the now and again of now I have you, the good wish
gone sour, the metaphor of love in place
of passion.

Let's note all of this. And the trees were lovely by the trail
today; they kept dropping leaves, filling whole coves
in the embrace of trees. Something keeps fulfilling
itself.

The world at a distance is showing off again. I don't know
  how to
do this, but the next time I love I will become an angel.

The Visibility of Angels

The night chokes on dank air, the last
hard air of summer. There was a terrible sunset,

the blood-red clouds sugared by a fold of smog.
Bryan and I sat on the balcony, amazing talk of
summers in the country, the full stars, the temperatures
shaking one day from the next. And there was talk of
love, how it enters the thin ribs of wanting and then
blows away, demanding nothing, leaving the spaces that
    kill.

We could have talked all night. But knew better. Believing
in footsteps that go home to a bit of brown shack,
to a fancy bedspread, to the caves that silence makes for
    itself; the hard
window looking into itself.

I am left here Bryan, with so much talk gone useless.
The good grace of forgetting how the heart tries for itself
and falls flat. Picking up the heaven from it is no
big deal; the experienced hands have faith that nothing
can beat the cold bones short of the grave.

There is a little nugget of hate on my left arm; through
all my patience at scraping the bones clean, the nugget
    shines
like a small star that mesmerizes me at night. It explodes
slowly in a lifetime.
There is nothing to keep me from a cave of its own light.
There will be you and I, still sitting and talking,
all ten fingers intact, a little sleepy,

there is no talk of the country, the blood-red smog
is a natural thing. In the last grasp is a swollen heart
we keep praying to for a change-over, another believing,
hounded out of life by the labour of loving it.

Relic

The cranes keep mouthing the plum of the afternoon.
The cicadas have gone to sleep, the light is
heavy and sick of itself.

I am rushing off now to a place no one has heard of.
A place of a cave of diamonds, in which my body breathes
itself back to the mummy of another year.
A year in which I was held up by both my lungs
shaking like tiny leaves, to drop footsteps
I would save the rest of my life.

I have walked here, by the grace of my own forgetting.
There is no other way to seem alive.

The Jump on Death

I'm going to charge this one up, the old machine, the stop
and start thing, the heart;
christ it's taken it this long to make the music,
it's taken this long for the castle, the air,
the music in the throat, the lump washed out
that is a summer in disguise.

I've got words to make this map out, following the breath
down every channel, the blood down every artery,
the words down every teardrop. The words have it.

I say them on a Monday afternoon, or on lonely nights,
under the arch of trees, the moon dimpling its way
across the mouth of a star – I say them, hey loser,

hey son of man, stalling out another
terror, you've everything to make up for, you are the
no-stakes winner, the need to make good in a house of bone,

the thankless operation of making the heart stand on its
 head.

Aquila

you want to get rid of these
little harpies

you want to confess they aren't yours
take the one called song
the way it turns everything you say
into gold
take the one called love
the way it brings out the best in you

get rid of them
there is the real you, ugly and taloned
with eyes like an angel
ready to eat the world
for the first time

Canzone

I can't get over tulips this month, they mouth
the sides of fences, taking a wrist-hold on
a clump of sun, and sing it out in my veins, those
beautiful little critters, rose-lipped, those
darlings that hem my life.

And when the world comes apart at the seams,
not the prettiest sight, I pretend a dance
that's made by loosening the heart from the head,
a fancy gesture, not at all becoming,
made to make death a little old with running off
at the mouth.

I do not want to believe for a moment the
way life takes pot-shots at the running children,
sinking their feet into the earth-well of the grave;
head first, the poor babies scream right through
the years until they land, small ghosts of pining,
on an average bed, on an average morning, eating
the breakfast of your lies.

I am done with it. This song tastes of dust,
the lake can never wash it through. My mouth
sings and it is all the same, whether in this
room or in that temple; it is the sound of the
lungs clapping to make up a hope; a way of breathing
the eyes back into god, a way of touching the rose
in the lover's hand, without telling him the hairs
of that peachy
world, his heart, are burning.

A Dreamer with the Usual Hands

You must approximate the stars,
the high heaven in a nutshell; the love of one man
for a woman, the high regard for last year's hell;
the plaintive love of the next good thing, love them,
they are the nearest you can get to heaven.

I remember the way I used to put one shoe on before
   another.
Now I leap into them, from the highest mountain, from the
far end of a lonely grave, from the deft touch of a woman's
palm, I leap into them, blessing the whole mad air;

And I used to believe in madness, and now I believe
how one man raises a tear the length of his head, his brain
washed out until he has nothing but a love for a leaf falling,
the way the air takes the sun at sundown, the way children
fill the playground like sparrows, the way two lovers
lean their heads together in October.

At night, I fall out of bed. I fall over and over,
backwards and forwards in the dark. I am a little boat
washed between four walls. I am rocking forever; it
is the body refusing to remember anything.
I've packed away the luggage for the night. Oh I know about
the sun, and the blades of grass in April, and the way the
   world

starts again in a thousand places.

It is the vertigo of staying alive for how many years.
It is making a big splash between two stars.
It is rolling up to that idler, god, the bones carpeted out of
the will to live.
Outside, three dozen leaves are falling out of the maple tree;
in five colours again, dammit, with no heartbreak, they are
   falling.

Passaggio

It is time I announced my desire to be a field,
a stone with one arm, a blue wind rising.
All the boxes of the heads of my friends
exploding, but gathering at dusk, after the fanfare
of sun and shadow. I am a little tired of the fireworks
over the lake, the confetti of cars, the ribbons
of a lover's tongue. It is time I announced that
the grave I walk in is not mine. I change it,
as of now. If you follow, you will have to dance.

At Home in Heaven

And you begin again by saying everything, up to the lonely
    trees,
up to the drop of water on your chin, you spout everything
and everything nods. It is high time you came out of the
    body
of men, the string of silences. It is time the body listened,
and the body hears itself;
these are the bones you have kept under cover for too long;
two arteries are singing. The scalp, the hairs, the wrists,
everything dreams itself, and you are saying. This is the
    way you

are, walk out into the sun, announce yourself to the body
of men, be a trumpet, be a sunset, be what god made you to
    be,

a bit of earth with a taste for saying, a bit of earth with
a verve for breath, a bit of leftover star with the shining
that won't come out, a bit of angel with paper for wings –

a man, with a taste for admitting it. This is the beginning of
everything, the power of hands for clapping and prayer,
the river tasting its own pebbles, the god, tying his own shoe

and falling off the chair.

The Unlimiting

Do you want to sing the moon, do you want to sing the
    white arm
of the rain; we can do either or both. I am tired of the lungs
    that had

that dream about blackbirds, and tried to get to heaven on
burnt candle ends. There is a carriage the size

of a man getting in, and wheeling himself to heaven. He has
    laughed
long and hard over other means of locomotion. He blew
    himself

up there once, on a breath. It was early in the morning then.
It is later. He has heard much talk about short-windedness.

Between one thing and another he figured out hands. For
    three years
he will figure out hands, at which time he will have a dream
of arthritis, and then he'll toe himself, or conjure his bones

into a cloud; he will go on doubting the return ticket while
    he makes it
to heaven and back, while the stones laugh, while the birds
    pretend to
be just starlings, while his mouth pretends to be just a
    mouth,

and all the while love preens its feathers, saying want me,
and the dream comes true.

The Sundays of St. Clair

These are the Sundays of St. Clair. December.
Coldness and the crispness. How many ways does a man
want to die, or sing or dance or take his pants off?

In a blue moon, a man is taking his pants off and he
is whistling all the while, he is whistling death and
love in the same breath, and he is doing it so well.

                                    In the middle of
the night I will get up and dance on the bedsheets,out of
love for two continents.

But now I will be quiet. I am going to say the rosary of
breath so quietly. Here: the way my mother sat by my
    father's bed
for months in the long-windedness of his death, the talk of
Antonino at four o'clock in the morning, my love for green
and purple flowers, the way a woman sings to me, now and
    again,

of children, of the Italian Alps,
and the long windings past my youth to a family of stars.

And I remember the dark highways, the ramblings, down
    one fledgling
heart, up another. And I remember how I could not
miss this much, all the world I have, not having known
    better.

Youngness devours itself, and dismisses heaven. It
    imagines everything
in a rain-drop, and holds nothing in the cup of its hand.

I am saying, Sunday. The Sundays of my life are returning
    themselves.
This poem could be called the name of gladness, but goes by
    the
name of a man walking himself home to find candles
    aflame. It is

the birthday of the things he loved, and when he comes
 through
the door his friends will rush to meet him, and he will give
them anything in the shape of gifts, but especially two eyes

that are a nod, a handshake, an embrace, and the moon
 comes down to
earth, and the man pulls up his pants, and goes to work for
 happiness.

Poem for My Friends and a Lady

I am belonging to the name of newness, to eyes that see themselves,
to hands that find the embrace and wink out heaven.
Imagine this, the poem that goes off and brags a little. Imagine
the little old men of the universities shaking at the name of this,

for they do not live inside this poem; this poem says all they
pushed backwards into the folds of their brain, the night they
dreamt cicadas, the love of them, and they ran off, hating the

sound of afternoons in their sleep. This is not for men who left
themselves on streetcorners, forgetting to sing.

I am belonging to the name of gladness, in the
final time, when the children return without the eyes of men, within
the heart they sit up and make fronds of everything. This is for

the lovers of children, who are children with a sunset on their
brows, with a taste for presents in their hands, with a need for newness in
every touch. This poem gathers up everything
we could have loved, saying we did, and for this we are ashamed of

nothing. We left nothing of it. It was the world that said
bye-bye and learned its lesson – so it goes dark at night, while

the children make of the stars something of a game, in which hearts
go back and forth, exchanging this, a love, which is a poem,

which is for you.

Who Will Hear of It

Everything recapitulates.
The eyelash, the song, and the tooth sat around discussing
 this,
and were amazed to step into a little man who fell in love
with you.

The moon and its forty-nine steps consider everything to be
 true to
your eyes, I say to you. But look at the slender hills, you
 reply.
Do you think I have need of that many kisses?

A Straw Hat for Everything

I open you, love, and the day comes out, a little broken,
with clouds for eyes. At other times I marry you in a box of
morning, and then we lie awake for noontime after
    noontime, for the
sound of crickets and the apples of sun in the left hand of
    the field;

finally, I find myself in a field my body opened, shadow
    after shadow
comes out, the body repeating its favourites. But by and
    large you
are the embrace of light going from one end of the avenue to
    the other.
In your sleep I have imagined this, or it was always so and I
    was busy
with the lint on my suit. Morning has such extraordinarily
    blue eyes,

and the telegram won't do, and I have always found myself
    to be a
little lazier than my smile.

Poem from the Night Before

Do you laugh because my existence is wound up over
   breakfast?
And so you find my poem. I am not overly enthusiastic about
my trumpets, they were always shaped to be a joy. But
   what is

marvellous is the return fever, the way you gather the
   apples
for my lap, and I polish them.

In a very round-about way, I am telling you I need you, and
   that
horse-laugh, death, spells everything wrong, even the leaves
   on the
trees.
   If I return now by the goat-path or the garden, the odour
of lilacs is there, the house that might be a peony, and that
spool, the brain.

The last will is the return to heroes. How they accumulate
   smiles —
one steps out of me, he will lose his way too. But we will
   leave
some roses for him at the bend, a bunch of them, and his
   eyes will

find the moon, by no accident.

How Happy Are the Flowers of Vermont

How happy are the flowers of Vermont, I shall save a little
talk for them, by the stones, by the droplets of water
by the cold ribbons of sun at the back door of autumn;

yes, and then again, I will love you. I don't want to think too
much about this, a kiss will do it.

I keep finding my hand tucked behind my back, when I am
 waving
flowers with the other. The village idiot is going to die,
I will see to it. Leaving only the smile. And we won't even
 try
to get wings out of it.

How happy are the flowers of Vermont. They hold their
 hands up
in the night. It is in none of the guidebooks. We will miss it
and it is right.

I have looked for you in a thousand states, but had to wait
for the falling open of the door of the ten ribs.

I could say, I found you in a cyclone in Nebraska. But
 everyone would say
his arm around her is like birds, a lake with an island in it.

Every night begins this way. My luckiness reaching to New
 England,
around Ohio, so it spends the night in Detroit, what of it?

And the fingers appear to be clouds, just clouds,
and the flowers of Vermont, I whisper to you in your sleep,
even they; to keep dawn a little miraculous, there is nothing
 I wouldn't
say.

And my arms around you. That poem, for
another time.

In amicizia

I think of my friends as arms-at-sides wonders, little
    thimbles
with their heads up in the clouds, little shufflers banging
into their baggage, and opening up shops in the sun. O
    serious
fantasticos, morning sticking to the ribs: you live in
aphrodisiacs, just to remember loving. You live in shoes so
as not to be conspicuous as angels. You live in letters that
never made it to a cloud. I surround myself with you
and ignore the spot in my brain that hurts, the easy throb;
something is lugging me from the spot in my brain

where cells have been kicked to resemble chairs, furniture,
    places
to rest. The rest of me is a throw-away amongst you. The
    dead ringer –
I want to land in the middle of my friends, and put up flags,
so that the dark men of Arcturus, when they find us, will
    think
of hearts: how human a way to have gone to have touched
    the stars.

The Request for Air

The light falls down, holding everything in its hands.
The sun widens its smile, hiding its shoelaces in a buttercup.

I am returning the world to its rightful owner,
the world that was on its knees. I'm sending it back where it
 came from –

and I'm returning with it. Half-way into the doorway of my
 ribs,
a man is waving the air in, like filling a room with
 butterflies.
He is out to make a field of several thousand arteries.
He is out to make several thousand arteries into a field, he
 is dreaming it.
He is making a field, and his head turns on the pin of his
 breath,

he is singing, he is singing all along, as I write this,

he is making manna of the cold bread of the body.

The Beaches, Lake Ontario

I love my friends, but I also love the people behind them,
lone wolves, smattering up to their walls like flowers
gone haywire, if you can imagine this, four people

wedged on the coast, on the beach, against the stars
on a July night, smoking the darkness, smoking like Indians
making vast signals to themselves, to wave their fortunes in.

Imagine, if you will, imagine, four lovers, lovers of earth
and good things that keep the heart warm in terror.
Tossing against the darkness, pebbles that whiten and
 explode
in the low water. Upstairs, there are 5 stars, 6 stars, a
 hundred,
falling in our mouths. We will make songs of that.

One is Peter. He will grow up to be a man with happiness,
and Wendy, she will grow up to be Peter's flower and make
a vast ocean of herself; 2 more are there,

one is a lover of moonlight, and crickets, the other lady
is a mad dash into his heart.

These are four prayers. Listen, if you will, to the sound
of hands rubbing the tinder of night. There is some talk
and laughter between them like cords, and between them
 there is
a filament spiders cannot make so thin. Like paper dolls,
the handholds they make are silhouettes against night's
 blackness.

I have a patience for this, this dumb defiance, and behind
the silhouettes the world is making supper of despair.
On the coast four people, friends, and one of them myself,

look at the people behind them; they are more
beautiful than what I say, and for that the stars will thank
them, one by one.

Driving to Point Pelee

Rolling in, mile after mile, with the
imperfectable one, the blue-eyed woman,

what do you think of the landscape announcing plantains,
orchards, pines, and the return ticket to Toronto, was it
    ever any
good, when by the side of the road, opening shops are the
    parts
of you that lived on wooden stumps; look there is a blue
    moon,

or is it the sun, a friend is holding the left wrist of a cloud,
and starts crying for happiness; then there is the blockade of

your lungs hanging between two heavens, it is irresistible
    and you laugh
at it. Meanwhile she is singing beside me in the car, she
    does
not know it, she goes by names, hosannah, matin, the palm
    with the
drop of rain on it in autumn. I think also that breakfast is
    a matter

of closing down smiles that look like darkness. We have
    arrived
at a place where birdcalls fill the marshes, and the lake
    washes
up to the land holding temperatures. A closet of ninety-
    degree heat
and another one, and the sun hanging its hat up in each of
    them.

I remember the way here. I left my shoes in an old town.
The wind was always ready to fall against my hand.

Quietly, I am telling her I love her. How she has the keys to
    every
closet door. The strand of hair I smoothed as she looked
    ahead, to the

white arm, to the dark city, to the old shoes – as I smoothed her

hair something came to me, a child, a bluebell, or was it the ribs,
finally and singly falling into place, and the heave, the long heave
to be with one another.

Birthday Gathering

All my friends come to the balcony, come to the balcony,
not Alabama, not Tuscany, they come to the door they come
 in,
coffee, the scent of grasses rising from the city; the hard fog
 clogging
the eyes of the skyline. A little old we are, and celebrating
 one of us.

It is my birthday. My turn rises, falls in their hands, they
 discuss.
I am the luckiest for now. We will take turns on each other
singing the ribs into place, like charmers of living.

All over the world, I will come back to this place, this night,
 handcuffed in the
heart of my friends. They will have me back tonight. I am
 the luckiest.
So
 says July the fifth. This is the practice of staying alive in
 a puffball,
this crystalline hour, these 24 fingers around the throat of
 my friends,

oh sweet garlands.

Voce di luna

I am the last man in the world at the end of time,
nothing amazes me, but the heart growing again, always, I will
be surprised by the growing heart walking around the streetcorner
sporting a new hat. Only yesterday it seemed to leave home,
to lose itself, now it's back, the son, and we have talks about
what it's been doing all this time.

Tonight I sat with friends, eating the food of talk, for six hours
we did nothing but explain ourselves over and over, with feeling
with nothing but a way to talk to flesh and blood; the way old men
under stars gibber of nothing special and argue at the wind,

we talked, and the moon grew full overhead, and the wind died down,
new morning and the new streets, empty at January's tail end;

we are going into tomorrow with a world for a face, with the heart
tied like a stone by a string behind us, tomorrow we will find
a place for it; it will explode; tiny parachutes with the hands of
friends will come down, they will shake hands with every
blade of grass and, for a moment, we will be happy.

Acknowledgements

Poems in this book have previously appeared in the following publications: *Tamarack Review, Storm Warning 2* (M&S), *Critical Quarterly, Canadian Review, Malahat Review, Contemporary Verse II, The Organ, Rufus, University of Windsor Review, Poetry Australia, Dreadnaught Press, Seneca Review, Dalhousie Review, Kayak, Confrontation, Waves, Queen's Quarterly, Miss Chatelaine, Voices International, Mosaico, Prism International, Grad Post, This is My Best (Coach House), Grain, River Bottom, Icarus, This Magazine, Poetry Toronto Newsletter, Books in Canada, Canadian Author and Bookman, Versus, Antigonish Review, DeKalb Literary Arts Journal, Dacotah Territory, Event, Process, The Poets of Canada (Hurtig), Jewish Dialogue, Review Ottawa, Canadian Forum, Origins, Wee Giant, The American Italian Historical Symposium 1978, Roman Candles (Hounslow Press), Multicultural DocuPak (J.M. Dent & Sons), Descant, Temple University News*letter, and *Italia America.* Special thanks to the Canada Council and Ontario Arts Council. Some of these poems were broadcast by CBC-FM, CHUM-FM, CJRT-FM, and ITV, Alberta. My warmest thanks to Dennis Lee for his editorial guidance and encouragement.

By the Same Author

We Are the Light Turning (1976)
The Sad Facts (1977)
The Circular Dark (1977)
A Burning Patience (1978)
Roman Candles (ed.) (1978)
Dancing in the House of Cards (1978)
Dolce-Amarro (1979)
The Tough Romance (1979)
A Straw Hat for Everything (1981)
Flying Deeper into the Century (1982)
Dark to Light; Reasons for Humanness (1983)
Women We Never See Again (1984)
Post-Sixties Nocturne (1985)
Virgin Science (1986)
Les Amours difficiles (1990)
(Translated by Frank Caucci)

Printed by
the workers of
Ateliers Graphiques Marc Veilleux Inc.
Cap-Saint-Ignace, Qué.